Prince and Rover of Cloverfield Farm

Helen Fuller Orton

Illustrated by Hugh Spencer

ESPRIOS DIGITAL PUBLISHING

Prince and Rover

of

Cloverfield Farm

✤

Helen Fuller Orton

"'What is his name?' asked Sue"

PRINCE AND ROVER
OF CLOVERFIELD FARM

BY
HELEN FULLER ORTON

*WITH ILLUSTRATIONS AND DECORATIONS BY
HUGH SPENCER*

1921

CONTENTS

ILLUSTRATIONS

FOREWORD

These stories are founded on memories of my childhood on the farm. They first took definite form in response to the requests of my own little boys: "Tell me about when you were little, Mama." Some of them were demanded over and over again; but it remained for Bobby, the youngest, to insist that they be "put into a book."

Many a time, after listening to one of them, he would say: "I wish you would write your stories, Mama, so that other children could hear them."

Always I replied: "I will try sometime."

But never did the time come when there were not other things to do.

Finally, one night, when I had finished telling, "How Rover Got the Cows out of the Corn," he said: "Mama, you always say you will write your stories, but you never do. Truly, I'm afraid the other children will never know them."

I looked up. There were tears in Bobby's eyes.

Did it mean so much to him? Would other children like the stories?

"Bobby," I said, "truly, I will try to write them. After Christmas I will begin."

So after the holidays were over and the older boys had gone back to college, the writing was commenced.

"Will they do?" said I to Bobby when he had heard the last story read. "Do you think a publisher will like them?"

"The children will like them," he replied.

So that is how Prince and Rover happened to be written.

H. F. O.

I

At Cloverfield Farm there were four horses—Dobbin and Bird, Dan and Daisy. Dan was getting old so he could not go fast or work hard any more.

"We need another horse," said Farmer Hill one morning. "Mr. Ross has some for sale. I am going over to look at them to-day and perhaps I will buy one."

"I hope," said John, "that you will get one that can go fast—faster than Daisy."

"I hope," said Sue, "that you will get a fine-looking horse."

"And I hope," said mother, "that you will get a gentle horse, one that will be safe for me to drive."

"I will try to please you all," said father, "but first of all we must have a strong, willing horse—one that will do his share of the farm work."

Father was gone all day, for Farmer Ross lived five miles away.

Toward supper-time Sue looked out of the window and exclaimed: "Oh, there's father with the new horse."

Just then Bobby came running in and shouted: "Father's coming with the new horse."

All three looked toward the road—mother and John and Sue.

Down the road was father in the buggy, driving Daisy while he led the new horse behind the buggy with a halter.

All the family went out to see the new horse when Farmer Hill reached the back yard.

"He is not as handsome as I had hoped," said Sue, "but he has a kind face."

"Can he go fast?" asked John.

"He is not a race-horse," said father, "but he has long, slim legs and can go over the ground pretty fast—quite fast enough for us."

"Is he gentle, so that I can drive him?" asked mother.

"Yes," said father, "he is a safe horse. He will not jump or run away even if you meet a threshing machine."

"I am glad of that," said mother. "Daisy jumps to one side if even a piece of paper blows near her."

"He is a good horse," said Farmer Hill. "He will not run away, but he is very strong-bitted and will have his own way sometimes. It would take a strong arm to hold him back if he wanted to run fast."

"What is his name?" asked Sue.

"His name is Prince," said father.

"That is a fine name," said Sue.

"I hope Prince will prove to be a good horse," said mother.

"He has one excellent trait," said father. "Farmer Ross says he always knows the way home. His daughter lost her way once and Prince found the right road and brought her safely home."

"What a wonderful thing!" said John.

"Now I will put Prince in the stall next to Daisy's," said father.

He went toward the barn leading Prince, while John and Bobby followed along.

When they reached the barn, Farmer Hill gave Prince a drink from the watering trough, opened the big door and led him into the stall.

In the manger were some oats, and the rack was filled with hay which he could eat whenever he wished.

So Prince had plenty to eat and a good stall to stand in. But he was not happy.

He kept thinking of his old home.

It was not nearly so big a stall as this and not nearly so fine a barn. The oats there were no better and the hay no sweeter. But that had been his home all his life, so he kept thinking about it and wishing he were there.

The fact was that Prince was homesick.

"I'll go back there if I get a chance," thought Prince, "and live in my old stall, with the horses in Farmer Ross's barn."

PRINCE SEES HIS OLD HOME

II

The next day after Prince came to Cloverfield Farm, Farmer Hill had to go to the city. He took Bobby with him and they were gone until afternoon.

All the other horses were out in the field working. Prince was standing in his stall, very lonesome.

He was still thinking of his old home and wishing he could go back there.

"I'll go back if I get a chance," thought Prince.

After a while mother said to John: "Prince must be thirsty. Father may not be back for some time, so I think you had better let Prince have a drink."

John opened the stable door and led him to the watering trough in the barn-yard.

All the while he was drinking, Prince was wondering how he could get away.

John had hold of the rope but not very tightly.

Suddenly, Prince gave a jerk and the rope slipped from John's hand.

Away went Prince, through the barn-yard gate, up the lane, out the gravel driveway and down the road.

The rope was dragging along, his mane was tossing and his heels went galloping over the dusty road.

By this time Farmer Hill and Bobby were coming home from the city in the buggy, and they saw a horse coming toward them down the road.

"Oh, father, someone's horse is running away!" said Bobby.

When the horse came near, father exclaimed: "Why, that is Prince! I must stop him."

"Whoa, Prince, whoa!" he said.

Prince never stopped but went galloping past.

"Oh, what shall we do?" asked Bobby.

"We must go after him," said father. So he turned Daisy around and they started after Prince.

"Get-up, Daisy, get-up," he said. He even took the whip from its socket and touched Daisy, just ever so lightly, but enough to let her know she must go fast.

And so they went down the road, Prince galloping along and Farmer Hill following after.

For two miles along a stretch of level road they went, Prince getting farther ahead all the time.

"I'll not let him catch me," thought Prince, "I shall run and run."

Then came a cross road and Prince turned to the right.

And so they went down this road, Prince galloping ahead, father and Bobby following after.

When Prince came to the next corner, he turned to the left.

Bobby saw him turn. "Prince has turned onto another road," he said. "Why doesn't he go straight ahead?"

"Perhaps he wants to go to some special place," said father.

By the time they reached the corner, Prince was out of sight around a curve in the road.

"Do you think Prince will run a hundred miles?" asked Bobby.

"We shall see," answered father. "Daisy is getting tired, so we shall have to go slowly for a while."

"Perhaps Prince will get tired and stop," said Bobby, "and then we can catch him."

But Prince had been resting in the barn all day, and his long slim legs felt as strong and fresh as when he started.

No, Prince was not tired, but he had reached the place where he wanted to go.

That white house just beyond the curve in the road was Farmer Ross's.

When Prince reached it, he slowed up, walked through the gate and down to the barn.

The hired man, when he took the horses out to work that day, had left the stable door open.

So Prince walked around to the back of the barn, through the open door and into his old stall.

"How nice to be here again," thought Prince.

When Farmer Hill and Bobby reached Mr. Ross's place, Prince was nowhere in sight.

They drove into the yard. "Why do we stop here?" asked Bobby. "We must keep going after Prince."

"We are going after Prince," said father.

"But Prince cannot be here," said Bobby. "He was galloping down the road."

"I think we shall find him here," said father. "This is his old home."

6

Father and Bobby looked around the yard, but no Prince was there.

The open stable door was not in sight.

Just then Farmer Ross came up from the field. "We are looking for Prince," said Farmer Hill. "He must have gotten out of my stable, for we met him coming this way and followed after."

"I have not seen him. Let us look around," said Farmer Ross.

But Prince was nowhere to be seen.

"Are you sure he came in here?" asked Farmer Ross.

"Not sure," said Farmer Hill, "but I think he did. Could he have gone into the barn?"

They went to the stable door and looked.

There was Prince standing quietly in his stall, eating hay from the rack.

"I told you he always remembered the way home," said Farmer Ross.

"I'll take him back and this time we'll be more careful with him," said Farmer Hill.

So again he led Prince home and put him in the stall beside Daisy.

Every day he fed him plenty of hay and oats, gave him a good bed of straw to lie on at night, and always treated him kindly.

John sometimes gave him a lump of sugar, but father always led him out to water and held the halter very tightly.

After a few weeks Prince liked the new home so well that he never wanted to go back to the old one again.

HOW ROVER
GOT THE COWS
OUT OF
THE CORN

III

Cloverfield Farm had a big Shepherd dog named Rover.

One day Rover lay under the apple tree in the back yard, taking his afternoon nap. Just over the fence in the pasture Farmer Hill's cows were grazing.

Suddenly Molly, the Big Red Cow, came near the stone wall on the farther side of the pasture. She smelled the corn in Neighbor Newman's cornfield beyond the stone wall.

Now if there is one thing that cows like better than anything else, it is growing sweet corn. Molly looked at it longingly over the stone wall. She smelled it in the breeze.

Not far away Molly saw a low place in the wall. Over this she jumped into the cornfield. All the other cows saw her and followed—the White Cow, the Black Cow, the two Speckled Cows, and the Little Red Cow.

They all began eating Neighbor Newman's corn.

Just then Mrs. Hill looked over that way and saw the cows in the cornfield.

Farmer Hill had gone to town that day, so he could not get the cows out of the corn. The hired man was down in the field by the woods, so he could not get the cows out of the corn.

"Who will get the cows out of the corn?" thought Mrs. Hill.

Going to the back door, she spied Rover taking his afternoon nap. "Rover, Rover," she called, "the cows are in the corn." But Rover only opened one eye a very little bit and wagged his tail, a very weeny mite, and went on with his nap.

Again she called, very loudly, "Rover, Rover, get the cows out of the corn, quick! quick!"

Rover understood this time and jumped to his feet. "Look, there they are," said Mrs. Hill, pointing to the cornfield.

When Rover saw what had happened, he ran just like a flash across the pasture lot, jumped over the stone wall and began to bark at the Big Red Cow.

"Bow-wow, bow-wow," barked Rover, which meant, "Go back into your pasture."

But the Big Red Cow only switched her tail and went on eating corn.

"Bow-wow, bow-wow," barked Rover again; but still she went on eating corn, and all the other cows went on eating corn.

Then Rover bit the leg of the Big Red Cow. It was only just a little bite, but she knew it meant, "Get out of the cornfield or I will bite you very hard."

The Big Red Cow went to the stone wall with Rover barking at her heels, until she jumped back into the pasture lot.

Then he went to the other cows and made them all jump back over the stone wall into the pasture lot—the White Cow, the Black Cow, the two Speckled Cows, and the Little Red Cow.

Just as the last cow was jumping over the wall, Farmer Hill came home along the road from the city. He saw what Rover had done.

Rover got back to his place under the apple tree just as Farmer Hill drove into the yard. "Good dog, good dog," said Farmer Hill in a kind voice.

Rover looked up and wagged his tail.

"Is there a bone for Rover?" said Farmer Hill. Mrs. Hill went to the cupboard and found a big bone and gave it to Rover.

"Rover made them all jump over the stone wall"

"I must have the men fix that hole in the wall," said Farmer Hill.

When Rover was through with the bone, he went back to finish his afternoon nap under the apple tree.

IV

"What are you going to do to-day?" asked Bobby one morning.

Father looked across the table with a twinkle in his eye.

"Prince and Daisy and I are going to help make bread to-day, Bobby," said he.

"Why, father," said Bobby, "you cannot make bread and horses cannot make bread."

"I did not say we were going to make it alone," said father. "I said we were going to help."

"Mother makes the bread. She makes it in the kitchen," said Bobby.

"But we are going to help," said father.

"Can Prince and Daisy come into the kitchen?" asked Bobby.

"No, they will not come into the kitchen," said father. "They truly will help, though. Would you like to see them?"

"Yes," said Bobby. "That would be fun."

"Come down to the field below the barn with me," said father.

So Bobby ran along beside father down the lane to the Old Red Barn.

Father harnessed Prince and Daisy, drove them to the field below the barn and hitched them to a tool with a shiny steel point.

"But, father, that is a plow," said Bobby. "Mother does not make bread with a plow. She makes it in a pan and stirs it with a big spoon."

"That is true," said father, "but we shall help to make bread with a plow."

Soon father started the horses while he held the handles of the plow so its shiny steel point would dig down into the hard earth.

Straight to the other end of the field they went, leaving behind them a long furrow of brown fresh earth.

Back they came toward Bobby, making another furrow. And so back and forth, back and forth, all the forenoon they went.

Bobby sometimes trudged along by father, sometimes he rested at the end of the field.

Bobby was watching very hard. At last he said, "Father, there is not any bread yet. When shall I see the bread?"

"It takes a long time to make bread from this brown earth," said father.

"Does it take all day?" said Bobby, who was beginning to get tired.

"Yes, it takes more than a day," said father. "It takes about a year."

"I think mother's way is better," said Bobby. "It takes her only one day."

"But mother could not make bread at all, if we did not help," said father.

"Oh, indeed, she does," said Bobby. "I have seen her make it all alone."

"Bobby," said father, "of what does mother make our bread?"

Now Bobby was only six years old, but he had often watched mother make bread.

"She makes it from flour," said he.

"What is the flour made from?" asked father.

"The miller grinds it from wheat," said Bobby.

"And where does the wheat come from?" asked father.

"It grows in the field," said Bobby.

"So far you are right, Bobby," said father. "Now look at the ground over there where I have not yet plowed. Would wheat grow if I sowed it there?"

"I suppose not," said Bobby.

"No, indeed," said father. "It would lie on top of the ground and wither and die; but when I sow it in the soft earth which Prince and Daisy have plowed, it will grow."

"Now I see," said Bobby, "Prince and Daisy do truly help to make bread."

"You are good horses," said he, patting them on their noses.

Just then the dinner bell rang.

"Come, Bobby," said father. "We will take Prince and Daisy to the barn and give them hay and oats. Then you and I will go up to the house and eat some of mother's nice bread."

"Oh, father," said Bobby, "you forgot. It is Prince and Daisy's bread too."

ROVER BRINGS THE COWS FROM PASTURE

V

Down on Cloverfield Farm the afternoon sun was sinking toward the West.

The swallows were coming home to their nests in the barn and a gentle breeze was starting the windmill.

Farmer Hill looked at his watch; then he went to the bars at the head of the long lane and began putting them down.

Rover, seeing this, came running up to him. "Yes, Rover," said Farmer Hill, "it is time to go for the cows."

Down the long lane trotted Rover, past the apple orchard, past the clover field, past the field of wheat stubble, to the thirteen-acre lot.

In the farthest corner of the field, with her feet in the cool water of the pond, was the Big Red Cow. Near-by, under the elm trees, were all the other cows lying on the grass.

Straight to the Big Red Cow ran Rover and barked. The cow knew what that meant. It said, "You must go home to the barn." So she started toward the lane.

Then all the other cows followed.

Rover came trotting along behind, barking sometimes if they tried to turn back.

So they all went up the long, long lane toward the old red barn—the Big Red Cow, the White Cow, the Black Cow, the two Speckled Cows and the Little Red Cow.

"'You must go home to the barn'"

Past the field of wheat stubble, past the clover field, and along the orchard fence, they went.

As they came near the harvest apple tree, the Big Red Cow smelled the apples. Now next to fresh green corn, cows like apples better than anything else. So the Big Red Cow tried to jump over the rail fence, to get some apples.

She might have gotten over; but Rover ran up to her and barked and snapped at her heels with his sharp teeth, until she started on again.

So all the cows went up the lane and through the bars into the barn-yard. They drank the cool water in the watering trough and then went into their stalls in the stable.

Farmer Hill turned to Rover and said, "Good dog, good dog!"

Rover wagged his tail very hard. He liked to bring the cows from pasture.

Then he went to the windmill to wait till the children should come with their tin cups to drink the nice warm milk at milking time.

HOW ROVER RESCUED LITTLE YELLOW CHICK

VI

Mrs. Plymouth Rock lived in the chicken coop out by the wood-pile with her brood of eleven chicks. There were black chicks and yellow chicks, but the nicest of all was Little Yellow Chick.

Mother Hen always stayed in the coop.

The little chicks would jump out between the slats and go off through the grass and into the driveway and among the chips of the wood-pile.

When Mother Hen wanted them to come home she would call, "Cluck, cluck, cluck, cluck!" and all the little chicks would come running to the coop.

One hot summer afternoon, Mrs. Hill was sitting on the back porch mending stockings. All the big hens were scattered around the place—some in the garden, some in the cornfield, some in the farmyard—scratching for bugs and worms.

Suddenly there was a great cackling and scurrying among the fowls. Those in the garden ran and cackled, those in the cornfield ran and cackled, those in the farmyard ran and cackled. They all ran as fast as they could to the hen house.

Mrs. Hill, hearing the commotion, stood up and looked around to see what was the matter.

There in the sky coming toward the farmyard, was a large gray hen hawk.

Old Mother Hen heard the cries of the other fowls and knew there was danger, so she called her chicks to come home. "Cluck, cluck, cluck, cluck!" went Mother Hen.

All the little chicks tried to run home to the chicken coop. They ran as fast as their little short legs could carry them.

Little Yellow Chick could not run fast. He tried very hard, but stumbled over a chip near the wood-pile.

The hawk up in the sky with his sharp eye saw Little Yellow Chick and flew straight toward him.

Old Mother Hen could not help Little Yellow Chick, for she could not get out of the coop.

Mrs. Hill ran toward him, but she could not help him for she could not run fast enough.

But Rover, lying under the pine tree in the front yard, heard the commotion and came running like the wind past Mrs. Hill.

He jumped at the fierce hawk and snapped at him with his sharp white teeth, just as the hawk was swooping to pick up Little Yellow Chick.

When Mr. Hawk heard the barking and saw Rover dash towards him he forgot about wanting to eat Little Yellow Chick and flew away as fast as he could.

He flew up into the sky and over the woods and far away.

Mrs. Hill picked up Little Yellow Chick and carried him to Old Mother Hen in the coop. Old Mother Hen took him safely under her wing.

"Rover snapped at him with his sharp white teeth"

"Good dog, good dog!" said Mrs. Hill to Rover as she patted his neck.

Mrs. Hill went back to mending stockings on the porch.

But Rover lay down near the hen-coop to guard Little Yellow Chick.

VII

The Big City was ten miles from Cloverfield Farm. Farmer Hill had to go there often on business. Mrs. Hill had to go there to buy shoes and clothing. Sometimes they drove, but if they were in a hurry they went to the village a mile away and took the train.

"I must go to the city to-day to attend to some important business," said father one morning. "It will not take long, so I will go down on the nine o'clock train and back on the eleven."

"Are you going to drive to the train or walk?" asked mother. "I need some groceries before dinner and wish you would drive so you could bring them back."

"I will drive then," said father. "I meant to walk."

Mother wrote down a long list of groceries—flour, sugar, tea, raisins, molasses, rolled oats and spices.

"I will leave the list with Mr. Brown," said father, "so he will have them ready for me when I come back and I won't have to wait."

So father drove Prince to the village and tied him to the hitching post in front of Mr. Brown's store.

He gave the list to the grocer.

"Please have them ready when I come back on the eleven o'clock train," said he.

Then father went to his train.

The grocer put up the order. "I might as well put them in the buggy for him now," said he.

So he carried the groceries out and packed them under the seat.

Farmer Hill intended to come back on the eleven o'clock train; but his business took him longer than he expected, so he could not come until the next train at one o'clock.

Meanwhile Prince stood very still and patient for some time. Then he began to take a few steps forward once in a while, and then a few steps backward.

Prince liked to go. He did not like to stand still so long.

Every time he stepped back and forth, the knot in the halter loosened a little. After a while, about one o'clock, it became entirely untied.

When father got off the train, he was still thinking of his business in the city and was in a hurry to get home. So he never once thought about Prince, but struck off across lots and hurried home afoot.

"Where are Prince and the groceries?" asked mother, as father came into the house.

"Prince and the groceries?" said he, "Prince and the groceries? Sure enough, I did drive Prince down this morning. I entirely forgot him. He must be standing at the hitching post in front of the store. I'll go back and get him."

Before this time Prince was quite hungry. He was very tired standing still so long. He wished he could go home to his stall and eat his dinner.

Still Farmer Hill did not come for him.

The next time he stepped forward, there was no halter to stop him; so he kept on walking down the street.

The thought of home and his dinner made him want them very much.

So he began to trot.

Just as Farmer Hill was leaving the house to go after him, Prince turned into the yard.

"There is Prince now," said father. "He has come home alone."

"But I need the groceries," said mother. "I must have the sugar right away. One of us will have to drive back after them."

"Sure enough," said father, "I'll go because I am the one who forgot them."

He started to get into the buggy.

"Why, here are the groceries," said he. "Prince has brought them home."

VIII

On Sundays at Cloverfield Farm Rover always stayed at home to guard the place while the family went to church.

Just once, a long time ago, he had followed clear to the church door, when Mr. Hill had sent him back home.

One Sunday in summer, father hitched the horses to the big carriage and drove up to the horse block where mother and the children were waiting for him.

"Did you lock all the doors?" asked father.

"Yes," said mother, "and all the windows too."

"Where is Rover?" asked father.

"He is under the apple tree," said John.

Then they got into the carriage and drove to church—father, John and Sue on the front seat; mother, Bobby and Baby Betty on the back seat.

Past two farm houses, under the Big Trees, past two more farm houses, down the little hill and through the village they went to the big stone church on the brow of the big hill.

After father had driven the horses and carriage under the shed at the rear of the church, all the family went into church and up the middle aisle to their pew near the front.

Meanwhile at the farm Rover was having a good nap under the apple tree.

Suddenly he was awakened by the sound of wheels on the gravel drive. Up he jumped and ran up the driveway to welcome the family home.

But what was his surprise to see a strange horse and carriage and strange people in the carriage!

"Strangers must not come into this yard when the folks are away," thought Rover. So he ran toward them, growling and barking.

"Bow-wow, bow-wow," barked Rover, "bow-wow-wow, gr-r-r-"

"Hello, Rover," said a man's voice.

"Why, I have heard that voice before," thought Rover.

Then he ran nearer and saw that the man was Uncle James and the lady beside him was Aunt Polly.

Rover stopped barking and growling and wagged his tail very hard and looked pleased, for he liked them.

Uncle James got out of the carriage and went to the front door.

He rang the bell and waited a few moments, but nobody came. He rang it again, but nobody came.

"I thought somebody always stayed at home with Baby Betty," said Uncle James.

"Perhaps some one is in the garden or out in the orchard," said Aunt Polly.

Uncle James hitched the horse, and then they looked in the garden and in the orchard, but could find nobody.

"Where are all the folks?" asked Aunt Polly of Rover.

"Find Bobby and Baby Betty," said Uncle James.

"'Strangers must not come into this yard when the folks are away'"

Rover pricked up his ears and opened his eyes very wide. He looked from Uncle James to Aunt Polly.

"Go find Baby Betty," said Aunt Polly.

Then Uncle James and Aunt Polly went to the front porch and sat in the big rockers.

Rover started down the road toward the church. He trotted along quite fast past the two farm houses, under the Big Trees, past two more farm houses, down the little hill and through the village to the big stone church on the brow of the big hill.

The front door was open, so he went through the vestibule into the big room where the minister was preaching.

"Bow-wow, bow-wow," barked Rover.

Farmer Hill looked around quickly, for he knew Rover's voice.

When Rover saw Farmer Hill's face, he ran up the middle aisle to the pew where the Hill family sat.

When they heard a dog bark in church, some of the boys snickered and some of the girls laughed and some of the older people smiled, but Farmer Hill put his hand on Rover's head and said very softly, "Lie down, Rover."

So he lay down in the aisle with his head resting on his front paws and kept very still all through the service.

When meeting was over, the minister came to Rover and patted him and said, "You behaved nicely in church, Rover."

As they were driving home, John said, "I wonder why Rover came to church."

"Perhaps he was lonesome at home alone," said mother.

"Perhaps something is the matter there," said father.

As they came into the yard, Sue was the first to see the visitors.

"Why, there are Uncle James and Aunt Polly," she exclaimed.

"Didn't Rover tell you that we were here?" asked Uncle James.

"So that is why he came to church, is it?" said mother.

"Rover is an intelligent dog," said father.

Rover looked from one to another and lay down on the porch where they were all visiting together.

PRINCE HELPS MAKE ICE CREAM

IX

It was the middle of winter and Cloverfield Farm was deep under snow. The ponds were all frozen over and even the little brook had stopped babbling and was frozen into silvery ice.

Bobby liked the winter, because he could coast on the Little Hill and take rides in the big bob-sleigh.

There was no work to be done on the farm in winter; so Prince and Daisy stood all day in their stalls in the Old Red Barn.

"How would you like a long sleigh ride to-day, Bobby?" asked father one morning.

"I'm ready for one; that would be great fun. Where are you going?" answered Bobby.

"Well, harvest time has come," said father. "So Prince and Daisy and I are going to help harvest butter and ice cream."

"This is not harvest time," said Bobby; "harvest time is in the summer when it is very hot. And besides, Prince and Daisy cannot make butter and ice cream. Mother makes the butter, and John freezes the ice cream."

"Do you remember, Bobby, how they helped make bread?" asked father.

"Yes," said Bobby.

"If you will come with me, I will show you how they *do truly* help to make butter and ice cream too," said father.

"Shall I have to go far, father?"

"Yes, it is quite a long drive. Ask mother to bundle you up warm," said father.

Before long, father was at the door with the big bob-sleigh drawn by Prince and Daisy. He tucked Bobby in warm and snug with the buffalo robe, and then away they went. The bells on the horses jingled merrily as they went skimming along over the snow.

"Are we going to the city?" asked Bobby.

"No, Bobby, not this time. We are going to the river," said father.

"I never saw any ice cream in the river," said Bobby.

"Keep your eyes wide open, Bobby, and you will see Prince and Daisy help get ice cream from the river," said father.

When they came to the river, Bobby could see that it was all one mass of ice. Men working there had swept the snow off and were cutting the ice into great blocks.

"Oh!" said Bobby, "this is where we get the ice for John to put in the freezer."

Father drove close down to the edge of the river and the men filled the sleigh with a great load of the big blocks of ice.

"May I have a dish of the ice cream to-day?" asked Bobby.

"Not to-day," said father, "not until summer."

They were on the way home now, the horses going slowly with the heavy load.

"But it will not be summer for a long time," said Bobby. "By that time the snow and ice will all melt."

"This ice will not melt," said father, "even when spring comes and the snow goes off."

"That is strange," said Bobby. "Truly I am afraid it will melt and then we shall have no ice cream."

"Just watch," said father, "and see where I put it."

When they reached home father drove to the ice house.

"Look in there," he said to Bobby, "and tell me what you see."

"I see a great pile of sawdust," said Bobby. "You won't put the ice in there will you, father? I do not want sawdust in my ice cream."

"We will see that no sawdust gets into the ice cream," said father, "and yet we could not make the ice cream without it."

Father carried the big cakes of ice into the ice house and piled them in rows on a deep layer of sawdust. Then he went for another load and another and another. All that week he kept drawing ice until the ice house was nearly full. Over the top of the ice and around the sides of it he packed sawdust until it looked like a mountain.

"Are you trying to keep the ice warm?" asked Bobby.

"No, Bobby, I am covering it with the sawdust to keep it cool," said father.

"That is very strange," said Bobby. "Mother puts blankets on me to keep me warm. You put a blanket on the ice to keep it cool. I think there must be a mistake somewhere."

After a few months spring came and the snow melted and the ice on the river melted.

One day mother said, "If you will get me some ice we will have ice cream to-day. I am going to churn too and will need some for the butter."

"I am afraid the ice is all melted, mother," said Bobby.

"Come with me and we will see," said father.

So they went to the ice house. Father climbed on top of the mountain of sawdust. Bobby climbed after him.

Father dug some of the sawdust off, then said, "Now you may dig, Bobby."

Bobby began to scoop the sawdust off. Pretty soon his hand touched something cold. He dug some more and then came to a piece of shiny silvery ice.

Father lifted it out. There was a large cake of glittering ice just as they had put it in last winter.

"Now we'll wash the sawdust off," said father.

So they stopped at the well and washed it all clean, and then broke it into pieces. Part of it they took to mother to keep the butter cool; part of it to John to freeze the ice cream.

When the ice cream was frozen and Bobby was eating a dish of it, father said, "Well, Bobby, who made the ice cream to-day?"

"I see now," said Bobby. "We could not have had it on this hot day if Prince and Daisy had not drawn the heavy loads of ice last winter."

"And I could not have made such good butter without the ice," said mother.

"If horses liked ice cream," said Bobby, "I would give some of mine to Daisy and Prince."

X

This is a story about Prince when he was naughty. It was one time when Farmer Hill let him out into the pasture for a day and Prince would not come back at night.

It began when Farmer Hill said one Sunday morning in spring, "I will turn Prince and Daisy into the pasture to-day and let the other horses take us to church."

All winter long Prince had been in his stall in the barn, except once in a while when he had been driven to the village or the city.

He had been standing in the dark stall so long that when Farmer Hill turned him loose in the pasture, he felt very strange.

At first he just stood near the bars and nibbled the short fresh grass. Then he slowly walked around to the clump of trees in the middle of the lot and ate some more grass; then he went to the far corner and took a drink of cool water from the little brook.

The sun was shining brightly, the birds were singing in the trees. Prince liked the bright sunlight, he liked the gentle breeze, he liked the fresh grass.

"I shall stay here always," thought Prince. "I should like to run and kick up my heels."

So he kicked up his heels and ran to the other end of the field.

After a while he went galloping back again.

All day Prince and Daisy were out in the pasture, sometimes eating grass, sometimes resting under the trees, sometimes running and prancing around.

Toward night, when it was time for them to go back into the stable, Farmer Hill came to the bars and whistled.

They both heard him whistle.

Daisy came running toward him, and he opened the stable door and put her in.

But Prince did not come.

Instead, he turned and ran to the other end of the field.

"I shall not go into the stable tonight," thought Prince. "I shall stay here always."

"He acts as frisky as a young colt," said father. "I shall have to put a halter on and lead him."

So he took the halter from its peg near the stable door, and walked toward Prince.

Farmer Hill had almost reached Prince, who had been standing quite still, when suddenly Prince kicked up his heels, gave his mane a toss and was off like the wind.

"Whoa, Prince," said Farmer Hill.

Prince did not stop until he reached the other end of the field near the barn.

Farmer Hill came back toward him, and once more Prince stood still until he was almost there and then bounded off.

"It is like a game of tag," said Bobby, who had been watching by the bars. "You never can catch him, father."

"I will fool him," said father. "I shall catch him then."

"How will you do it?" asked Bobby.

"Just watch, Bobby, and you will see," said father.

Father got a measure of oats from the granary and walked toward Prince, holding it out to him.

When Prince saw the measure of oats, he wanted some to eat.

After a while he started to walk up to the measure. Then he stopped.

"I will not go near him," thought Prince. "I will stay out in the pasture."

But the more he thought about the oats, the more he wanted them. After a while a bright idea came to him.

"I will go and take one bite," thought Prince, "and then I will run away quickly."

So he walked slowly up to Farmer Hill.

Farmer Hill let him put his head into the measure.

Prince took one bite. That tasted so good that he took another and another until the oats were all eaten. While he was eating, Farmer Hill slipped the halter around his neck.

Then he tried to get away, but the halter held him tight.

"I have you now," said Farmer Hill. "You must come into the stable."

As father led him to the stable, Bobby said, "Prince was naughty that time, wasn't he, father?"

"Yes," said father, "he led me a merry chase, but I cannot blame him much. Who would not rather be outdoors on a day like this than in the finest stable, or house either?"

"I think Prince was sensible," said Bobby.

ROVER DOES SOME MISCHIEF

XI

Cloverfield Farmhouse had a new looking glass. It was a very large looking glass, reaching to the ceiling and almost down to the floor. It was in the parlor between the front windows. On the little shelf under it were two beautiful vases.

Rover was not allowed in the parlor except once in a while. One Sunday John let him come in and lie in the corner.

After a while all the people went out of the parlor. Rover was there alone fast asleep. When he wakened, he looked all around the room.

Then he got up and walked around to find a door.

There between the front windows was surely a door into another room.

Rover saw himself in the looking glass, but thought it was another dog coming toward him into the parlor.

He began to bark at the other dog. But the other dog did not go away. He even barked at Rover.

Rover went nearer and the other dog came nearer too.

Then Rover barked louder and showed his sharp white teeth. The other dog showed his sharp white teeth too, but did not go away.

Rover barked and barked, which meant, "You must get right out of this house." Then he ran at the other dog very fast.

He ran so fast that he bumped his head hard on the looking glass. He knocked over one of the pretty vases and broke it into a hundred pieces.

Mother and Sue heard the crash. Father and John heard the crash. They all came running into the parlor.

There, among the broken pieces of the vase, was Rover still looking savagely at the dog in the looking glass.

John pulled him away from the glass. Mother said, "Bad dog, bad dog!" Sister Sue scolded him and opened the door and put him outdoors.

"Rover looked savagely at the dog in the looking glass"

"Rover was fooled that time," said father.

"We must not allow him in the parlor again," said mother.

Rover knew he must have done something wrong. With his head down and his tail hanging very limp he went to the horse barn to lie in the dark corner and think it over.

XII

"Where is Baby Betty?" said mother, coming up from the cellar where she had been making butter.

"I saw Baby Betty's pink sunbonnet in the front yard by the maple tree an hour ago," said big brother John. Then he ran to the front yard and looked everywhere—behind the maple tree, under the lilac bush, down by the road, but no Baby Betty was there.

"I saw Baby Betty down by the pump not long ago," said father. Then they looked by the well, and in the corn crib and all through the farmyard, but no Baby Betty was there.

"I saw Baby Betty's curly head in the garden a while ago," said big sister Sue. Then Sue ran to the garden and looked under the currant bushes, behind the asparagus bed and in the strawberry patch.

But no Baby Betty was there.

"Where, oh, where is Baby Betty?" said mother. Then they all looked, down the lane, in the apple orchard, in the clover field and behind the haystack, but no Baby Betty could be found.

Just then Rover came home from the village with the hired man. "Where is Baby Betty?" said father. "Find Baby Betty." Then he showed Rover Betty's little pink sunbonnet. Rover smelled of it and looked around the yard and whined. First he ran to the front yard and then to the pump, then to the garden and then to the strawberry patch beyond the garden.

"He thinks she is in the strawberry patch," said Sue, "but I looked there and I surely would have seen her."

Up and down the rows went Rover, and across to the farther side of the patch. Soon he stopped and barked a little and then came running back.

Again he started over to the strawberry patch. "I believe he wants us to follow," said mother.

Then all of them followed Rover away to the farther side of the strawberry patch.

There, behind a clump of tall plants, with her hand clutching some ripe berries, was Baby Betty fast asleep.

Father lifted her and carried her to the house. Mother came close along by his side; while John and Sue patted Rover's neck and said, "Good dog, good dog."

Rover looked up at them with his kind eyes and wagged his tail very hard.

Baby Betty went to playing again in the yard, and Rover lay down under the apple tree to watch over her.

PRINCE SEES A DRAGON

XIII

"May I have a horse to drive to town this afternoon?" asked mother one noon in summer. "I must take Bobby and Betty to get them some new shoes."

"Yes," said father. "You may have Prince to-day. He is our safest horse."

So Sue stayed at home to get supper, while mother and Bobby and Betty went away in the carriage toward the city.

The city was ten miles away. It was a pleasant drive, past the little red school house, past farmhouses and orchards and cornfields and woods.

When about half way there, down the road in front of them there appeared a big threshing machine, with its engine drawing it along.

"Chug-chug-chug-chug," went the engine. Slowly it came toward them.

"Do you think Prince will be scared?" asked Bobby.

"I hope not," said mother, "but you had better take fast hold of Baby Betty so she will not tumble off the seat if he jumps."

"Chug-chug-chug-chug," slowly came the engine.

Prince pricked up his ears.

"Whoa, Prince," said Mrs. Hill, "steady, Prince."

"I'm not afraid of that," thought Prince. "I have seen that thing before. It makes a lot of noise, but it never hurts me."

So he went along steady and easy past the threshing machine.

After a while they came to a railroad crossing.

"I will look down the track and you look up the track," said mother to Bobby.

"I see a train coming," said Bobby.

"We will wait until it goes past before we try to cross," said mother "Whoa, Prince."

So Prince stood facing the track.

On came the train, very fast. "Chug, chug, chug," went the engine. "Toot, toot," went the whistle. "Ding, dong, ding, dong," went the bell. Soon the train went whizzing past.

Prince did not jump. He just stood still and looked at the train as it passed. You see, he had seen trains many times before.

When the train had passed, Mrs. Hill drove over the track and on to town.

After she had bought the new shoes for Bobby and Betty, they started home again.

Just as they were going down Main Street, along came a parade with a brass band at its head. "We will stop here and see the parade," said mother.

When the band came near them it played very loud. The drums were beating, "rub-a-dub-dub, rub-a-dub." The horns and the fifes and the flutes and the drums, all made a beautiful big sound.

Prince pricked up his ears.

"I have heard something like that before," thought he. "It never did me any harm."

So he stood very still as the band went past.

After the parade had gone by, they started toward home.

"Prince seems not to be afraid of anything," said mother.

As they drove along, Bobby was silent for a long time.

At last he said, "I know what this is like, mother."

"What is it like?" asked mother.

"To market, to market, to buy a fat pig. Home again, home again, jiggity jig."

"Only this time," said mother, "it is, To market, to market, to buy some new shoes. Home again, home again, what is the news?"

It was almost dark by the time they passed the little red school house.

Suddenly in the road ahead there appeared a strange object, coming straight toward them. It sounded something like a steam engine. "Chug, chug, chug, chug," it went.

In its face were two great glaring eyes.

"I never saw one of those before," thought Prince, "but I shall not jump."

On it came toward them very fast.

Just as it was almost there, it went "honk! honk! honk!"

Prince pricked up his ears. Mother held tight to the reins. "Whoa, Prince; steady, Prince," she said.

Prince did not mean to jump, but he had never seen anything like that before and he was just a little scared. Just then the strange thing went "honk, honk," close to his ears, as it went whizzing past.

Before they had time to think, jump went Prince to one side, which made Baby Betty slide off from the seat.

"'Whoa, Prince, steady, Prince,' said she"

"What was that?" asked Bobby.

But mother did not answer, for Prince was pulling hard on the lines and going along very fast.

"It must have been a dragon," thought Bobby.

Though mother pulled on the reins as hard as she could, Prince did not slow up, for he was a strong-bitted horse and did not mind mother's pulling. He went fast all the way home.

When he reached home, Prince just slowed up of his own accord and went trotting slowly into the yard.

Father was waiting by the horse-block to help them out.

"What fine new shoes!" he said. "What is the news?"

"Prince jumped and ran when he saw the dragon," said Bobby.

"The dragon?" said father. "Did you see a dragon?"

"Yes," said Bobby, "and it hissed and sputtered and went 'squawk, squawk,' very loud and had two great big eyes."

"Oh, that must have been one of those horseless carriages," said father.

Bobby shook his head.

"I am quite sure it was a dragon," said he. "Prince thought so too."

XIV

It was a cold winter's night at Cloverfield Farm. Outdoors the snow lay deep on the ground. The cows and the horses were warm in the Old Red Barn. The hens and chickens were safe in the warm hen house. The pigs were snug and warm in the pig pen.

Inside the house a big fire was burning merrily in the sitting-room stove. A fire was burning in the kitchen range.

All the family had gone to bed. Rover had been allowed to sleep in the kitchen that night instead of in the cold wood shed.

In the middle of the night the wind blew hard and made the kitchen fire roar up the chimney. It became hot—so hot that the wood around the chimney began to smoke and burn.

All the family were asleep upstairs. They did not smell the smoke. They could not see the flames.

But Rover was awakened by the smell of smoke and the crackling of the fire. The smoke made his eyes smart. He knew that something was wrong, so he began to bark.

But nobody heard him and nobody came. Then he ran into the dining-room and barked, but nobody heard him and nobody came.

He went to the door of the hall which had been left open just a little. Up the stairs, barking and barking, went Rover.

Farmer Hill heard him, and thought, "What is Rover barking for?" Mrs. Hill heard him and said, "Something must be the matter. Let's

45

go and see." John heard him and jumped up and ran down stairs. Farmer Hill and Mrs. Hill ran down stairs.

Then they smelled the smoke and saw the fire.

Mrs. Hill grabbed a pail of water and threw it on the fire.

Mr. Hill went to the cistern pump and pumped a pail of water and threw it on the fire.

John ran out to the well and brought a pail of water and threw it on the fire. Sue brought snow and put it on the fire.

All together they worked, and soon the fire stopped blazing and went out.

"If it had not been for Rover, the house might have burned down," said Farmer Hill.

"Rover is a good dog," said Mrs. Hill as she patted him.

"Good dog, good dog!" said John and Sue.

They gave Rover a nice warm blanket to lie on, and fixed the stove so it could not draw so hard.

Then the family went back to sleep.

Rover lay down on the blanket, but he did not go to sleep.

All that night he kept watch.

XV

One day in summer Farmer Hill said at breakfast, "I must go to the city to-day. There are many things to do, but I'll be back before dark."

Then he hitched Prince to the carriage and started off along the road, down a long hill, over the little bridge at the foot of it, along miles of level road to the city.

All day he was going about his errands, while Prince stood in a stable and ate his dinner and rested.

Toward night, just as Farmer Hill was going to start home, a thunder storm came up. It thundered and lightened and rained and rained.

It rained so hard that the water ran in the street like a river.

Farmer Hill waited until the storm was over. By that time it was nearly dark.

There were no street lamps along the road.

There was no moon in the sky.

There were no stars in the sky.

It became so dark that Farmer Hill could not see more than three feet ahead.

"I shall have to let Prince see for me," said he.

Prince trotted along over the muddy road, now and then slowing up when he came to a pool of water, now and then turning out when they met another team.

Finally they had come back as far as the foot of the hill where the little bridge was.

"Now I shall soon be home," thought Farmer Hill.

Just then Prince stopped stock still.

"Get-up," said Farmer Hill. Prince did not go. "What is the matter?" thought Farmer Hill.

He tried to look in front along the road, but could see nothing.

Just then a flash of lightning came and lighted up the country around for a moment.

"Why! the bridge is gone!" said Farmer Hill.

Sure enough, the heavy rain had made the creek so high that it had swept away the little bridge.

"If your eyes had not been better than mine," said he to Prince, "we should have been thrown into the water."

Then he turned Prince around and went back along the road to the corner and took another road home.

At last, very late in the evening, they came to the farm.

"I am glad to be at home at last," thought Farmer Hill, as Prince turned in at the driveway.

Again Prince stopped.

"What is the matter now?" thought Farmer Hill. "Surely, there is no bridge gone here."

"Get-up," he said to Prince. But Prince did not go ahead; instead he backed.

"'Why! the bridge is gone!' said Farmer Hill"

It was so dark that Farmer Hill could not see the horse; he could not see the trees; he could not see the ground.

"Get-up," said Farmer Hill again.

Prince started forward; but this time he turned out and went on the grass at the side of the driveway.

"I wonder what can be the matter there," said Farmer Hill.

John and mother were waiting for father and came out on the back porch as they heard the wheels coming.

"We were afraid something had happened to you, it is so late," said mother.

Then father told them how the bridge was gone and how Prince had refused to go on.

"But I cannot understand," said he, "why he would not come into the yard by the driveway."

"I'll go and see," said John.

John took the lantern and went down toward the road.

In a moment he came running back.

"Come here," he called. "That big flash of lightning must have struck here. There is a great hole in the ground."

All ran to look.

There in the driveway was a deep hole with the gravel and earth and big stones thrown about in all directions.

"And Prince could see that in the dark!" said father. "Twice he saved me from harm."

"He has wonderful eyes," said mother, "and he used them well."

"I shall give him some extra oats and a lump of sugar," said John.

THE END

Lightning Source UK Ltd.
Milton Keynes UK
UKHW010638200521
384056UK00001B/79

9 781006 985850